GUMBO

BY THE SAME AUTHOR

Gabriel

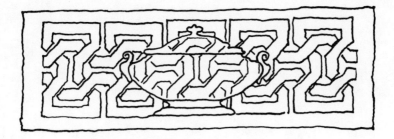

GUMBO

George Barlow

1981

Doubleday & Company, Inc., Garden City, New York

DESIGN BY RAYMOND DAVIDSON

Library of Congress Cataloging in Publication Data
Barlow, George, 1948–
   Gumbo.
   I. Title.
PS3552.A6725G85   811'.54
ISBN 0-385-17529-9
ISBN 0-385-17530-2 (pbk.)
Library of Congress Catalog Card Number 80–2557

The National Poetry Series

1981

Gumbo by George Barlow (selected by Ishmael Reed)
The Dollmaker's Ghost by Larry Levis (selected by Stanley Kunitz)
Leaving Taos by Robert Peterson (selected by Carolyn Kizer)
In Winter by Michael Ryan (selected by Louise Glück)
So This is the Map by Reg Saner (selected by Derek Walcott)

In memory of
Robert Hayden, 1913–1980

CONTENTS

Gumbo:

a soup thickened with okra,
shrimp, crab, sausage,
chicken, filé, etc.

serious eats of the lip-smackin,
shell-crackin, soul-moanin variety

choice greaze in a big pot

the food of the spirits

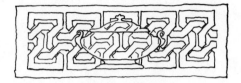

PART ONE

Gumbo

Little fishes in the brook,
Brother catch 'em with a hook,
Mama fry 'em in the pan,
Papa eat 'em like a man.

EULOGY: *Adiós Adiós*

What might he say now
about life & its particulars
How might he sum it all up
Where might he tell us
to look for the truth
about things

Guess he'd tell us
to scrap our lofty notions
altogether
Tell us in plain & simple terms
that life is what it is:

a day at the track
Tanforan   Bay Meadow   Golden Gate
a racing form in your fist
a long shot   a good nag
a hearty sprint
from gate to wire

a white carnation
in a pinstriped lapel
in the middle of the Great Depression
Tweed cologne & a manicure
a gray felt brim
& silk socks
spit-shined shoes
& a watch that works
a new green Impala
a sunny day & all the honey
in South Berkeley

a mirror that agrees
with you a phrase
that feels good on your tongue
sounds good in your ear
becomes you
Adiós Adiós
Hold the phone
Hold the phone

Maybe he'd say
it's about keeping your clothes clean
& your wits about you
in Oakland's old "bucket"
or dreaming about owning
a chain of liquor stores
that could wrap
around the world ten times

Or maybe it's about
being a railroad man
& holding the magic
of "the mole"
close to your heart
knowing what it means
to be long gone
down the tracks

the easy speed of a night train
conjure in the names
Challenger   Shasta
The City of San Francisco
Sunset Limited   San Joaquin Daylight
taking good care of the big shots

taking good care of your family
best of everything for the big shots
best of everything for you
& your family

Or maybe it's about
being the best cook on earth
storming your niece's kitchen
on Sunday afternoons
& watching a perfect turkey
emerge from the hurricane
a mess of wild rice dressing
& cranberry sauce
candied yams rolls & string beans

Or clowning
signifying
whirling in a bottle of good sherry
your face flushed & moist
your heart dancing
to its own dizzy beat
Hold the phone
Hold the phone
Adiós Adiós

knowing the special vanity
of a short light-skinned
Louisiana man
thumbing his nose
at old age
being stubborn with style
impossible & irresistible
honery & wonderful
refusing to go gently

splashing simplicity & complexity
into a shot glass
belting them down
& smacking your lips
realizing your uniqueness
& celebrating it
Adiós Adiós

knowing why folks do what they do
knowing that
you're the only one like you
knowing how to turn
good times into great times
Hold the phone
Hold the phone

Maybe he'd say
it's finally about
loving & being loved
knowing that folks you've touched
will never forget you
that they'll
pull in their memories
from time to time
like a big fish net
& celebrate each detail
keep you warm in their hearts
& sharp sharp sharp
as a tack in their minds

for August Merrell Richards

TITTA

Mama said they called you *Titta*
& loved you

She said that you would go crabbing
on Avery Island each morning
& picnicking at Camp Knighton
in the summer

That your salt held things together
when my grandfather
a handsome young doctor
collapsed in the kitchen & passed
into his dream of a fine brick house
for his family

That you came to her one night
after they had buried you
& stopped her crying because
everything was gonna be all right

Titta she said means *sister*
woman of New Iberia
sister of the South woman of the bayou
hot sauce & mystery in your veins
myths & songs in your voice

I see you now in an old photo
a giant oak behind you
a creole sun on half your face
Mama Auntie Vet & Brother
clinging like leaves
in the background

And when we gather to eat
our marriage birth & death
I troll the depths of heavy black pots
crack open the past
with my teeth & fingers
chew its tender legends
breathe your name
in the gumbo air

GAS

My woman says it's gas
in my daughter's belly
that makes her flash
a quick smile
from time to time
I say it's magic & love

Deranged from no sleep
bright images of an easy birth
oozing in & out of my head
I sit rocking my firstborn
a tiny rosebud
only eight days old

From stereo grooves
in a jam on the box
Cannonball cuddles her
softly in jazz
in the warm wings of Birdland:
alto lullaby alto love

Soulfully he blows
"Two Sleepy People"
& my eyes stop burning
as the budding little flower
smiles quickly in her sleep

It can't be gas:
has to be magic
Cannonball & the sweet horn
love & her papa's
rocking heartbeat
that makes her bloom

for Erin

SEARCH

How many times
has bad luck
shrugged our shoulders
& crooked our eyebrows
over lost photos
or shutters never snapped

How many times
have we locked our smiles
& pressed on to other
family feats & fragments

When I've asked you
to conjure him up you've
pointed to faces in crowds
movies or posters: "There now,
he looks like Daddy . . . *there*
is your grandfather"

You've shown me
Emiliano Zapata all of my uncles
Walter Brennan & others
You've tried

Maybe a candle of his love
flickers behind your eyes
& makes you see him
everywhere

makes you snuggle up
next to your memories
when you go back
to get him for me

Daddy's little angel
you said he called you
Daddy's little angel

Maybe I should look for him
in your eyes
lit in their details
shining in their reminiscence

for Yvonne Elizabeth Fisher

LITTLE HALF-BROTHER, LITTLE BLACK STAR

When I see him
gliding gazelle-like
stealing the white
out of third base

pulling a fly ball
from the sky
like a star from
his very own galaxy

bobbing his bushy head
to a new beat
digging the ancient sorrow
of an ancient song

taking his breaths
his cuts
his love
& his freedom

I see
runagate blacks
stealing their way
by the north star

&
cosmic blood
running through his
night train veins

& a woman
we found
some time ago
in an old family bible

Harriet
an aunt of his
a black woman
they called *The General*

for Mark

NOOK

Our speech slurs now
Tickled in our
wet paralysis
we let smiles tremble
on & off
our lips & cheeks

Now it's hard to tell
where I end
& you begin
Lost myself somewhere
back in our dance

Now our eyes
leave themselves shut
& our limbs slowly dissolve
as a lifesaving breeze
comes down from the curtains
above our wreckage

The earth can turn
without our help
We won't be missed
on the freeway
& the stock market
shouldn't crash
just because we've spent
all we have
on each other

for Bobbie

SALT

The bay breeze
licks at your
coffin & flowers
as it moves
over these hills
& through our family

Sunglasses shield
ashen cheeks & gutted eyes
breaths come
almost naturally now
as the wounded earth
takes you in

The loss
the numb heaviness
of things
unsaid unfinished
has settled quietly
on our shoulders
& planted us firmly
on this hillside with you

Your stickpin spirit
your diamond heart
your salt
help us bear the weight

Here is love
that is oak willow

poplar pine maple
luck conjure style
in these cradle roots
for you forever
precious uncle

MAIN MAN GONE: MOURNING POEM
FOR DADDY

Gone   Gone   Gone
    These gray mornings
    have no meaning
    beyond the thick drive
    from home to work—
    Oakland to Treasure Island—
    but now the fastened windows,
    the soft Naugahyde
    & padded doors
    of the Pontiac
    constrict him.
Gone   Gone   Gone
    Now the cars that
    slowly inch their way
    through the dense flow
    are metallic worms
    that will soon
    move through Andy's
    skull, ribs & joints
    on mornings like this.
Gone   Gone   Gone
    Now the bridge,
    with its rivets
    & sterile angles,
    is a worn kidney machine
    pushing his man's blood
    through him
    to keep him alive—
    painful living;

dry-skinned pain;
painful cleaning;
tacks & shrapnel
through his veins & arteries.
Gone   Gone   Gone
The muffled groan
of the engine,
the sporadic flash
of brake lights
in front of him
push Andy
up into his throat
& tighten his face.
The medical whine
of dialytic workings
stopped last night—
quickly & totally.
Gone   Gone   Gone
Andy is gone
in the clock on the dashboard;
gone among the paperclips
& pencils on the seat;
gone in the nervous
pedal-shifting
of a spit-shined shoe
& the numb control
of power steering;
gone in the distant thumps
beneath the car,
the heaviness of the sky,
the chill of the bay;
gone in the damp license plates
& mist on the windshield.

Gone   Gone   Gone
    He's gone, gone;
    wheeled into
    Kaiser's deep freeze;
    gone in the air
    that fills this lost morning,
    these trembling nostrils,
    this broken chest.

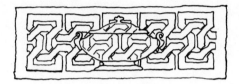

PART TWO

It's a Purple World

If they box you on the curve, boy,
Jockey your way to the rail—
And when you get on the inside track,
Sail!   Sail!   Sail!

(A Toast)

THE PLACE WHERE HE AROSE

it's about style
in the afternoon sun:
purple satin jumpsuit
white gangster hat
white platforms
& a pose

brother-man be out there
dead up in this corner
gonna be here a while

& why not
cause it's about style
& people be profilin

he ain't no linear dude
so why should he
stroll between
the white lines
of the crosswalk
just cause
the light jumps green

fuck the light
it's about bein scoped
in the sunday sun
it's a purple world

one bus passeth away
& another bus cometh

but brother-man
abideth forever
the platforms also gleameth

check out
the dapper dude
'bout clean as the board of health
dressed back is
the masai man
the jack-o-diamonds
the last mack

dig this man
in his satin threads
dead up in there
always been here
he is
what it is

for Quincy Troupe

FACING THE PRAIRIE

deep in her pupils
    the black hills
    red willow bark
    in the pipe fragrant air
    a bonnet
    resolute hoops & plumes

& the keen hunkpapa lance
    honed in the sun
    stands looking back
    from the ridge of her nose

& in her delicate cheeks
    variegated rawhide boxes
    the easy breath of eagle-wing fans
    beaded bands hanging from lakota braids
    a pony ghost-dancing
    on the undulating
    bluestem wheat & buffalo

& over her chin
    the powder
    the little white
    the prairie
    where reeds & songbirds
    flute the sturdy heritage
    of painted sons & daughters

& at her mouth
    where history & lyrics live

& the wish beams
a sunfast sunkissed rosebud
parting its petals
to the great sky

for Nancy Fast

OF THE BIRDS & THEIR EXUBERANT ACROBATICS

Quickness & cunning
will & nerve
my hurt & my madness
have brought me here

I ease across
in a battered old Volkswagen
& wave back
at border guards
too white.   too busy
with tourists
to see me

Brutal   canine   official
they wave
from their post
undetecting   unseeing   unaffected

My poems banned
my life banned
I ease away from my soil
like a ghost
haunting & haunted
Sharpeville a lead ball
on my heart
Port Elizabeth
a brick in my gut

Only my brothers
see me leave
only my brothers will miss me

for Dennis Brutus

OLD MAN SWEEPING

I drive through zero
each morning
Look for me

in the primal vacuum
between one moment
& the next

I come & go
in the
A.M. magic show

Commuting magicians
only vanish
only to appear

more like
the doughnut's hole
than the doughnut itself

everywhere & nowhere
more abstract than
a left turn

more absurd than
a right
nothing really nothing

I move from here
to there
& read the signs blindly

My speed is checked by radar
I merge left my right lane
is closed ahead

I usually see no kinship
in the clock-punching mugs
a fat man

true smoke
swirling in his cockpit
a woman yawning desperately

a car-pooler
catching his rightful winks
in the back seat

nothing nothing
mad transit &
a lane change

a truck bearing down
& the glass eye of the CHP
nothing nothing

But this morning's
light has caught me
in front of Mickey's Blue Room

where an old man
is slowly pushing a big broom
through last night's hoopla

Cold cold morning air
chill in his face
& hands

How many magicians
have vanished
before him this morning

He seems
unaware of me
unaffected by my gaze

Maybe he was young once
Maybe he glanced over
at an old man once

on a cold morning
like this
& thought he saw his life

run quickly down
a broom handle
like a mouse

Maybe he squashed
the vision in the same instant
with a blink of his eye

Now he sweeps
& doesn't his floppy old hat
tattered fatigues

slow careful moves
make more sense
than

my clock
my steering wheel
my corny routine

34

Isn't he past
present
future

the chill
that clutches
my idling bones

the light that
will change in a moment
naturally absolutely

He is

SPOUTING HEARTS SPOUTING MINDS

The pistol snaps
matter-of-factly
close to the
young guerrilla's head

He's a washcloth now

He goes limp
falls
practically in slow-motion
like in the movies

The spout goes up
from just behind his ear

Some Americans could
drink from such an arch
by simply leaning forward
simply taking the blood in

BOOK REVIEW: QUICKSKILL ON THE WING

How can anybody
have they little toes
in 1977
& they big toes
in 2000
& one heel
in 1861
& the other heel
in 400 B.C.?

       Hell
I know somebody
walk around like that
all the time

       Some things
just don't seem possible
(grabbing-globs in the frig
two-headed doctors
bingbuffers
moogies
sap moving nasty
on trees what
jes grew
& champagne cocktails
on antebellum
jumbo jets)

But one never know
do one

                             for Ishmael Reed

TOYLAND TOYLAND: VIDEO POEM FOR BOYS

boys
get g.i. joe
with kung fu grip
he'll crush your nuts
& rip your hip
tear your flesh
& crunch your toes
bust your lip
& break your nose
squeeze your guts
& gouge your eye
& clutch your throat
until you die
& clutch your throat
until you die

SOUL SOUL SUPER BOWL
(A POEM EVIDENTLY FOR DUANE THOMAS)

Evidently, Duane Thomas
    is a badassed brother.
Evidently, the brother
    was the Super Bowl. . . .
    runnin thru/around/under/over
    Dolphins all day long . . .
    shootin hoodoo thru the middle,
    whippin mojo on the score board,
    sweepin blues on blue Dolphins
    right & left . . .
    runnin amuck & not givin a fuck.
Evidently, Duane Thomas
    is a beautiful dude.

Evidently, the beboppin/flipfloppin/
    ragmoppin/fingerpoppin
    Dallas lockerroom ain't doin much
    for one white boy's nerves:
    the sweat on his face,
    shirt & sportscaster's sport coat,
    the tremor in his network voice
    & the tremblin mike in his hand
    all spotlight his stone fear.
Evidently, he's all wet
    & scared shitless cause

he gotta interview Duane Thomas
& he don't know if he can deal/cope
with a crazy brother like him:
    "Well, Duane, there's been
    an awful lot of talk about your
    strength, agility & speed . . .
    That was quite a show you put on today . . .
    Tell me, Duane, is Duane Thomas
    as fast as some have said?"
Duane say, *evidently*—
Don't say nothin but, *evidently*—
Say it quick cool & mean—say *evidently*

Evidently, this white boy
    expected a whole lotta
    bullshit TV jocktalk
    cause he got to sh-sh-sh-shakin
    & uh . . . uh . . . stut . . . stut . . . stutterin
    & carryin on—
    started diggin deep down
    in his TV bag of tricks
    trying his damndest
    to find some kind of way to deal
    with this crazy arrogant brother
    who *evidently* ain't sayin
    nothin but *evidently*,
    who's *evidently* talkin
    straight out the middle of his mouth,
    who's *evidently* got the audacity
    the gall the blazin unmitigated crust
    to answer the question
    he was asked with *evidently*.

Evidently, Brother Duane
 don't know how
 to shuffle his football cleats
 in the champagne & dust
 on the lockerroom floor
 don't know how to grin
 a big Uncle Remus grin
 into the camera
 & say, "Hi, Mom!"
Evidently, Brother Duane
 speaks English & Badassed Niggaese,
 is a razor blade & burp gun,
 a cheetah & a night-train
 or the brightest baddest star
 in the Texas sky, or just
 a beautiful beautiful dude.

AMERICAN PLETHORA:
MacCorporate MacDream

come come come
to the mustard & the ketchup
the pickles & the lettuce
come together   come to us
for macmiracles & maclife
we will macknowledge you
come   believe

follow our clown through
the great golden arches
he'll do it all for you
the world is a filet-o-fish
a quarter pounder with cheese
a raspberry shake with fries
believe believe

we'll mince the idea
with the onions
spread the notion
on the egg macmuffins
spike the coke with the vision

believe believe
that when you sleep
you'll macdream
when you wake
you'll macstretch
macbrush your teeth
& come come come
to us for coffee

james brown
kate smith
the carpenters
& fleetwood mack
will macsing our macsong

come come & sing
our rare destiny
look to the macfuture citizens
macsteak & maclobster
salt & pepper
for your souls
cream & sugar
for your bodies
come come come

we're the biggest macs
on earth
machustling the world
from the back seats
of our long black maccadillacs

all all
all we macwant is maceverything

ICE CREAM

It oughta be a law
about the way
she be eatin
a ice cream cone
& gazin out the window
when we be cruisin
thru Berkeley sometime
Make a person
have to stretch out his arms
& stretch out his left leg
& push his left foot
all hard against
the floorboard
Make somebody yawn
when they ain't gotta yawn
Make a man balls
squiggle around tween
his legs & everything
Make a brother
pull in his stomach
& then let it out again
Make a brother almost
run his fool self
thru a red light
& tear up his ride
It oughta be a law

WISDOM

if you don't
catch her
lookin at you sometime

like she wanna
just grab you
& eat you up

she don't
if you do
she do

STACADEMIA

Lot of folks
don't know it
but Stagolee
used to go to college

didn't like it
too much though
said none of them
professors & deans
seemed to have
they heads on tight

no style
stack said
wrinkled suits
& desert boots
no soul nowhere
punch-drunk pundits
lettered loons
that's what stack
called 'em

One day
Stack was sittin up
in a philosophy class
& the prof said:
 I am a liar
 I always tell lies
 & i am lying about
 being a liar
 now Mr. Stagolee

tell me how and/or
why my last statement
is true or false

Stack didn't say nothin
just reached in his pocket
pulled out his .44
& blowed the professor away
Said he was just
puttin the old fool
out of his misery
& doin everybody a favor

You know
ole Stack dropped out
the day before
they was to give him
his B.S.
in analytical euthanasia
& he never went back again

ELEPHANT ELEPHANT: LOONEY TUNE

FOR MITCH

Ya know George
I've been thinkin
& I think
I know just
how I wanna go
when it's time

I wanna be
ridin high
in some pussy
I mean
just really gettin down
& just when
it really starts gettin good & poppin
& makin all them
old funny noises
I want a giant elephant
to come through
the wall
& step in my back
before I even
know what's happenin

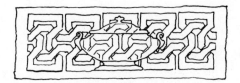

PART THREE

*Parchester**

* *A black village situated on the*
east bank of the San Pablo Bay
at the northernmost tip of
Richmond, California

NAMING AFFECTION

one black boy
can be
a cowboy a plum
a brother a man
a baby a dude
a home a junior
a boots a son
a george a barlow
in the warmth
of familiar kitchens
porches backyards
driveways hearts
& bellies

THE RAFT

maybe we called it
the *raft* because
it wasn't a body
we could define

not lake not pond
not river not canal

maybe its nondescript glint
floated on our
kneepatch minds until
a raft crystallized

who knows?

all that really mattered
was the big hills bros. can
full of nameless polliwogs
& the slow holy walk home
& the mud-funky tennis shoes
& the biology
of the next few days

HONG KONG

He was Hong Kong
of the giant shoulders
long arms
wine eyes
& black pepper whiskers

tall-taller
painter of houses
moon jester
from the grassroots
gracing our colored streets

He was Mr. Robinson
Mr. Hong Kong
whose whole-souled stride
hearty presence
& love of the glass
helped us make
our connections

No doubt he strode
this earth before
He was Li Po
the old Chinese poet

who would sit with wine
absent to night
& then stagger up
to stalk the brook's moon

We'd call him Hong Kong
& raise a vision
of divine lunacy
& simple abandon

I toast him now
as he drinks immortality
from a bottle
with a gentleman of leisure
in the mountains

A toast!   A toast!   A toast!
Again another for Hong Kong
gone on

INVASION: STRANGERS IN THE VILLAGE

They would roll in
on Sunday afternoons

a battalion
of dropped mercs & fords
        pink black candy-apple-red
        teardrops skirts rims
        chromed to the bone
        pipes poppin
        & James Brown screamin
        Bewildered from the radios

a low-ridin army
of konked heads
& do-rags
cuttin their wild
Berkeley eyeballs at us
& flashin
white port 'n lemon juice smiles
at our fine village women

Ashby
Russell
Sacramento Street niggas
out for juicy conquest
hopin the flames
in the names
on their fenders
will heat Parchester's panties

Prisoner of Love
Duke of Earl
Mr. Clean
Black Beauty
Green Monster
Heartbreaker
Fireball

THUMPIN

1.

Called him
too many
no-count niggas
so
a mad blade
sliced her right thigh
just below the hip

Quick clean slice
of love & marriage

We could hear
her clear scream
echoing in the
eucalyptus trees
that guard
the golf & country club

A wounded bride
in the leaves
& branches
giving us the blues

2.

He sits
in his driveway
bugeyed
deranged

staring at the broken stick
in his hand
completely unaware
of the sobbing in the house
the clean fresh morning air
the dew on his trimmed lawn
the robed
slippered people
on the sidewalk
who've come to the noise

He sits in silence
as the storm
calms behind
his bulging red eyes

> (*Can't git ovah it—*
> *broke clean in two—*
> *Bitch sho got a hard head*)

3.

Damn, what happened?

    Zack did it.
What????
    Yeah.
How, man?
    Bessie hit him in the eye
    with a hammer &
    he snatched it from her &
    slapped her upside her head
    & ran outside &
    busted out all the windows

on it & tipped it up
on its side like that
What????
 Yeah.
A Coupe de Ville????
 Yeah, ain't that somethin?

4.

Fixed his ass good
she said

Said she just
took her time
gettin it ready

Wasn't no hurry
He was still sleep

Let it sit
& boil a while
then grabbed
some potholders
carried it
in the bedroom
& woke him up

I don't know
who called the police
& the ambulance

she didn't

BB GUN

Quit scratching
on his own
finish in a minute
sense his danger
& pull out

They know how
to get away
I thought in my half-sleep
blip   under the cabinet
blip   behind the couch

But he kept doing
my chest of drawers

I went through
his death
a billion times
before he died
I'd move catlike
one motion at a time
ease back the cover
& slip from the bed
lift the flashlight
from the desk
& grip my gun
at the trigger
creep to the drawer
snatch it open
blind him
& blast him

A BB in your brain
is what you get for scratching out
a nest for your family
in the middle
of the night

His surprise
pressed hard against
my eyelids
as I tried
to snooze through
the next four nights

Small brown spot
in my drawer
forever
BBs BBs in my dreams

SIGNIFYING PERFECTION

Alvin could stand
in front of his black house
& disappear
close his eyes
close his mouth
& disappear

Joel could pass
his slight frame
through a closed door
slip one of his flexed biceps
through a needle's eye
easily easily

The knob
on top of Arno's head
represented a peak
in human cranial development
the point being that
Johnny called him "Knobby"
for a reason

The outward curvature
of Melvin's legs
wasn't unlike
the outward curvature
of Venus   Earth   Jupiter   Mars
bowlegged bowlegged
to the bone

& I was told
more than once
that I could float
on the two boats
I called my shoes
size ten at fourteen
a nautical nigga
on the San Pablo Bay
floating with ease
natural Buster Brown ease

POPPIES

Sometimes
when I flash back
to the sun in their faces

the dusk in their eyes
the night in their fingers

the way they bloomed
brightly in barefoot
summer popsicle days

the way they intoxicated us
with love
& monkey bites
between the houses
& in dusty old sedans

the way they eased
their floral tongues
between our teeth
& pressed their tight petals
against us

I wonder how in hell
we could ever strut around
calling the young fine things
bitches broads who'es & hams

anything & everything
but what they were

black brown & yellow
poppies blooming
for our jive hearts
& hungry blue jeans
along the tracks
of the Santa Fe

BEING BIGGER

The need
would well up
in us sometimes
like a big sneeze
& petrify
our narrowed pupils
wooden knuckles
budding rhino horns

Our hearts embalmed
our brains ablaze
we'd charge the sun
the moon each other
being bigger
brick brows
hatchet heads
bigger bigger

GOOPHERED RAIN

Seems like
wasn't no regular rain
in the village
Sometimes it would
bojangle gently
on the roof
& cozy things up
enough to
make you squeal

Like it could
be so together
tappin out
a funky little beat
on the porch

so light & fine
so sweet & even
lovely doin its thing
with the grass & gladiolas

Like it would
invite you out
for a solitary stroll
drops here for your heart
drops there for your soul

& then turn around
whoooo-wap
& do a number
on you

run your ass
back home
send you slippin & slidin
around to the kitchen door
where it done
already let itself in

Like it could
be so mean
all sprawled out
like the devil
on the floor
frownin laughin lookin
up at you
& talkin shit:

> *Okay you silly*
> *wet goo-loshed sombitch*
> *I'm up in here*
> *go get the mop*
> *& some newspaper*
> *& deal with me*

PAINTING DRUNKEN TWILIGHT

I.

Waves the short two-by-four
in a slow circle
                    above his head
        Wobbles slightly
                    with each wide-angle
                            slow-motion step
            Mumbles drunken curses
                            in thunderbird tongue

Comes after them
as they run
                    down McGlothen giggling
looking back
            stumbling over each other
                    in popeyed excitement

In this Transylvanian twilight,
this dank gray middle,
they aren't little black children
but panicked Romanian villagers
scurrying over the cobblestones
with Baron Frankenstein's man
at their heels.

And they have seen the teeth
& heard
the heavy footsteps before.

2.

The old drama
is alive again
in the juba dusk.
The red eyes, broad brow,
& long slow strides are familiar.
He has smashed the machinery again
& broken out the laboratory walls;
emerged again
to eat palm trees, howitzers,
& power lines.

And he has seen the scurrying before:
knows the wide human eyes,
the screams & flight very well.

3.

It's an old song,
a long vital dance,
an ancient film
flickering behind our eyes.

See how worn the celluloid is.
You know each frame
by heart.
Run with the little urchins
as you ran then; pump your knees high
& fly with them.
Glance back over your shoulder
& let the old fear—
the old thrill—
sprint through your arteries.

Race with them
all the way back to Altamira
where you first
worked it all out
on a rough sandstone wall
with adhesive gum & pigments.
Race with them
& be thankful
for the muscular young drunk
behind you growling
& waving his arms
& plodding step by step
in his wrinkled coat,
baggy pants,
& dusty construction boots.

He comes
with the drama,
helps in the twilight play,
gets you all the way back there—
to your first scene.

NIGHT WALK

There is conjure
in the bay wind
moaning through
these streets tonight

guinea pepper cat-bone
conjure woman wind
licking my face
dancing on the flat roofs
& sidewalks
doing a slow grind
in the treetops

haunting teasing breeze
pulling me down streets
with holy names
Griffin Bradford Jenkins Payne

Goophered stars & juju moon
light my way
past dark windows
& sleeping toys in flower beds

In this ancient village
this swamp magic
voodoo night
parked cars are crocodiles
sleeping with their eyes bucked

An empty beer can
spooked by the wind
rolls itself
out of the gutter

A drowsy watchdog
lifts his German nose
for my scent
as I walk along

hands stuffed snugly
in my pockets
following the conjure woman
through the dark-skinned night

Conjure conjure conjure
in the village streets tonight